ETERNAL DREAM

LEONARDAS ANDRIEKUS

ETERNAL DREAM

SELECTED POEMS

EDITED AND TRANSLATED
BY
JONAS ZDANYS

MANYLAND BOOKS, INC.
NEW YORK

ETERNAL DREAM
Copyright 1980 by
Leonardas Andriekus

All rights reserved

Published by Manyland Books, Inc.
84-39 90th Street
Woodhaven, N.Y. 11421

Library of Congress Catalog Card No.: 77-72585

ISBN 0-87141-061-3

PRINTED IN THE UNITED STATES OF AMERICA BY
Franciscan Press
341 Highland Blvd.
Brooklyn, N.Y. 11207

This is my message to the world
That never wrote to me:
The simple words that nature told
In tender majesty.

Emily Dickinson

CONTENTS

SHORES OF OBLIVION

INTRODUCTION

Leonardas Andriekus was born in 1914 in Barstyčiai, a small town in northwest Lithuania called Žemaitija. After entering the Franciscan Order in 1935 he studied theology in Austria and Italy, from 1937 to 1941. He was ordained a priest in Milan in 1940 and in 1945 earned his doctorate in Canon Law from Antonianum university in Rome. While in Italy, Father Andriekus ministered to the needs of Lithuanians stranded in Reggio Emilia refugee camps. He came to the United States in 1946, became involved in the daily activities of the Franciscan Order, and during 1964-1969 served as the Provincial Superior of Lithuanian Franciscans in the United States and Canada. He was Chairman of the emigre Lithuanian Writers' Association in 1970-1980 and is currently editor of Cultural Magazine *Aidai* (Echoes). His published volumes of poetry include *Atviros marios* (The Open Seas, 1955),

Saulė kryžiuose (The Sun on the Crosses, 1960), *Naktigonė* (Night Watch, 1963), *Po Dievo antspaudais* (Beneath the Seals of God, 1969), *Už vasaros vartų* (Beyond the Gates of Summer, 1976), and a volume in English translation by Demie Jonaitis, *Amens in Amber,* published by Manyland Books in 1968.

The poet, in modern times, is something of an exile on earth who must pay the penalty of separation from the ordinary world for devotion to his art. Contemplative silence is both a product and a creator of solitude. The Lithuanian emigre poet suffers a double painful kind of exile and separation. Because of historical events and political forces beyond his control, he has been driven from the land of his birth and forced into the painful state of literal as well as metaphorical homelessness. The poetry of Leonardas Andriekus reveals a man who has suffered through, and survived, both kinds of exile. Though the anxiety of displacement, symbolized by the untamed wind and the restless sea, often inhabits his poetry, Father Andriekus has managed to find relief for his ravaged conciousness and spirit. The fright, doubt, questioning, and often-paralyzing insecurity which exile brings pose the danger of a poetry of nostalgia or of nihilism. Father Andriekus expresses those emotions in his poems, and is often tortured by them, but in the end he transcends them and avoids despair because he realizes that the true home of both the literal and metaphorical exile is God.

Religion, the life of the spirit, offers solace to the man who has witnessed the agonies of the Eastern European experience. But, the religious passion expressed in these poems is distinctly non-sentimental, one which avoids the easy platitude and the empty adulatory phrase and is marked by a spiritual toughness little interested in expounding dogma or laying down the rules of practical morality. There is a mystical

X

quality to these poems, a sense of constant revelation of God as the One who, in turn, reveals Himself in all the living and growing things of the earth and in the "harmony of the birds and stars." It is through such a realization, Father Andriekus tells us, through the discovery of the kinship between God and man and nature which knows no national or ideological bounds, that even the agonies of literal and metaphoric homelessness and exile can be transcended and overcome. At times wry, sometimes pious, always accomplished, this is a poetry of hope and reaffirmation carved out of the black experience of anguish and pain. It occupies a unique position in the history of Lithuanian literature and, as such, it certainly deserves recognition by the English-speaking world and a well-lighted place in the gallery of modern European verse.

I have selected for inclusion in this book those poems which, even in translation, best reveal the range of Father Andriekus' thematic and formal concerns. I was aided in the selection by Father Andriekus himself, and I wish to express my warmest thanks to him for his assistance and cooperation throughout the translating of this book. Others who deserve a warm note of thanks include my parents, Alfonsas and Janina, for their help in translating some of the more difficult lines and phrases; and my wife Genovaitė, for her perceptive comments and her very special steadfastness and support.

Jonas Zdanys

THE HEART OF POETRY

The first blossom glistened with dew —
The rest of the world will soon flourish . . .
Sing, Ikhnaton,
Sing, Francis of Assisi —
Once again the sun,
The heart of poetry,
Rises from the night!

There are no thorns
Or spear wounds
In that heart —
It is open to our song of joy
On this side of the morning,
And to your voices
Beyond the gates of time.

You do not know, poor man of Assisi,
You cannot feel, King Ikhnaton,
How much I would like
To be reborn a blossom,
To call myself brother of the sun —
To lose myself in the melody of morning . . .

You are my Father

CHILD

Sit me down in the mountain grass
The way you would an orphan child
And leave me — I will be protected
By the wings of flying birds.

Put a golden dandelion in my hand
And let me play with its petals —
Laugh when the wind chases the day
Across the sighing autumnal fields.

I like that yellow sky,
The child's smallness, the earth's dread,
The millions of flying birds,
The dandelion in my hand.

I know You will protect
The child in the grass
When the black bird tries to strike him down,
When the wing of night touches the flower.

5

THE HARMONY

You give me
Whatever I pray for,
As if you cannot say No
With lips seared dry
By the burning of suns in the crosses.
You inspire the words of the prayer,
Take pleasure at the harmony
Of the birds and stars.

I ask little —
You yourself know
That the spirit brims with love
Like a tulip that has inhaled
All of the nectar of the morning.
Today the oceans and hills
With which you dizzied me
Rang out like a song.

6

The holy fires will fall
From the stars.
Birds will carry the embers in their beaks
To the tulip chalice —
To my sung-out soul.
You divide your treasures,
I rock in joy
On a reeling wave.

Take pity,
Bend the wings
Of the weakened bird on the road
Like you bend the wave
In your ebbing sea.
You are my father, I your son —
I always drown those embers
With my tears.

7

SEVEN RIVERS

In the other life the seven rivers
Met only in the sea.
Evening embraced them,
Holding a crown of bloody thorns.

The rivers are fortunate to have escaped.
But we remained here,
Helpless near the seven dry furrows,
Fingering the sands.

Christ's blood is on those thorns —
Sunset, do not be filled with pain!
Someone repents there, face pressed
Against the seven shores . . .

Somewhere an oasis rises,
Water spurts through rock —
The seven rivers in the seas
Sing a tuneless song.

ROCKS

I am no longer amazed that your fingers
Left their imprints on the rocks
When you touched them
That first creation morning.
Where would the willow tears fall tonight,
Where would they roll down the supple branches
If our rocks
Near the rivers and ponds
Were not marked
By the fiery imprints of your fingers?

I am no longer amazed that our willows
Are not sorry to shed their tears
When in the moonlight
Lilies exult in the rivers and ponds.
Where would the awakened stars wash tonight,
Where would théy bathe
If the willow tears
Flowed down the flat rocks
Into the damp grassland ground?

THE WANDERERS

Where were you, o my Lord,
Through that long night
When the wind blew out the candles
And the embers no longer burned?

Where were you yesterday when we cried out
Having lost our way?
Not a single errant spirit
Wandered through the fields.

The morning star in the sky had died,
The moon was not yet born.
The angry trees in the forests hurled
Harsh curses at the wanderers. —
They were disturbed by our sighs.

RIVERS

The slow flowing rivers
Of the land of our birth
Can't be blamed if, wakened by spring,
They seek the sea.
To the sea they carry blood and tears,
To the sea they carry your sighs, Lord —
And now they have deepened
My own great pain.

Even near their mouths
The river currents do not slow.
They carry many words of love
To the dark and terrifying depths,
They carried my longing,
Many shining sunsets of the spring.
And now I know
Why the ocean sighs,
Why the amber thrown to shore
Is so transparent.

THE OLD GRAVEYARD

If I am found unworthy
To enter the kingdom of peace,
At least remember, Lord, that I closed the gates
Of the old graveyard more than once —
As the wind tossed and banged them
And did not let the dead rest easy
After the labors of the summer and fall.

You understood their weariness once —
Their hot harvest, their cold threshing.
Those people left life calm and gentle.
Though they died in pain, they lie
With placid faces in the ground
Beneath their treasured wormwood trees.

12

With placid faces and tranquil hearts
They placed their heads on the fresh-cut sod
And died believing in eternal peace,
And so those graveyard gates were banged by wind—
So hard that in the ground
The heaviest coffin lids were lifted
And the crumbled dust in the coffins moved.

Lord, I rejoice that I braced shut
The graveyard gates with a rock from the road. —
Give me peace in your kingdom,
Give me eternal peace!

13

OASIS

How green you are, oasis,
How pure, how alive!
Where could I find such peace
If not in you!

The caravan passed by
Bearing frankincense, gold and myrrh,
And you remained in my Sahara,
Open to the miracle of this star.

14

The three travelers refreshed
Themselves at your shoreless river
And rode off to the holy city
In the name of the Lord.

I do not know what to call them —
Wisemen or kings,
But their sign will turn the stars
In new directions.

I began my journey
Without frankincense, gold or myrrh,
And found my own way across the deserts
To the city of the Lord.

SUNSET

This bloodfilled sunset
Promises nothing good —
Only a night without dawn:
With the emptiness of fallen stars,
With restless nightwatches,
With a painful glow.

I know all its promises,
The quick red flicker of flame
In the windows of home.
It will soon grow dark. Help me, Lord,
To drain this bitter cup
To the bottom.

It will grow dark. Change into an eyeblink
This long night without dawn,
Without love, without dreams.
Lord, fill the emptiness of the skies
With my grief,
Deepen the oceans.

I know that in the divine wholeness
Even the star that falls into the sea
Does not find only emptiness —
Let my grief engulf
This bloodfilled sunset
And this night without dawn.

17

MIRACLE

The land called Heaven revealed itself —
It was seen by God's chosen;
It was seen by the wild charlocks
Flourishing in the summer fields.

I hurried to the well
To wash the dust from my face,
And the Lord unlocked
The shell of each snail in the sea.

Each had enough air to breathe,
Each drank the joy of morning —
The earth became an altarstone,
The charlocks flamed like candles.

Who today would want to return
To the dark shells of the sea snails?
Like an infant after baptism,
I have been washed by the waters of grace.

18

WE THREE

We three traveled to the town of Emmaus,
I, you and he,
Lamenting that with us also traveled
Great sadness.

We were weighted with Golgotha's hill,
Defiled crosses,
The curse of our betrayed God,
Thirty-three silver slugs.

And we believed that we were equal
Children of the dark
As we walked farther from God's holy city
Along the paths of night.

19

And it was pure luck that we asked him
To spend the night at the inn
Just when that terror-filled sunset tried
To tear the three of us apart.

We found there wine poured by his hand,
The prepared fish,
And as he broke the bread we cried:
It's Him, it's Him!

SLEEPWALKER

You, who cure sleepwalkers,
Come, come to me —
I am lost in pleasant dizziness.

Come, not to heal or calm,
Not to place hands on my head,
But to warn the willows
Not to whisper my name.

Leave me in this happiness
Between sleeping and waking,
Bless the melody of this silver life
As it pours into my heart.

It's good to walk the rooftops,
To see the silent town beneath my feet,
And not know how long
You will let my shadow touch it.

Come, hold back my body
If the demon strikes to smite me —
The horrible abyss gapes below . . .

21

RESURRECTION

I know you raised Lazarus
From the dead,
And his weeping sisters
Soon quieted.
Why do the waves wail in the seas,
Why do my sisters cry out
There is no resurrection?

Does it matter that stones
By the sea's edge laugh
At my tears as they fall
On the hot sand?

With a song of anxiety, ripened in pain,
I will lift autumn like a coffin-lid
From the dead springtimes —
I will call back the skylark
To my fatherland's fields,
And in his voice
Each grain of earth will feel
The triumph of resurrection.

22

Again the night

THE SETTING SUN

Let's measure out the shadow with our steps;
We have enough time for our task.
It's not too early when the fall stops raging,
It's not too early when the sun turns white.

We will soon know how many steps
It takes to reach the coming shore of night.
Soon shadows will tremble in the valley
And the sunken bell will waken in the lake.

25

UNEASINESS

This twilight is calm,
Only stars fall,
Only rivers drone,
Only hearts tremble . . .
Someone may think
That there can be peace
Even in uneasiness.

He who stops
The stars and waters
Will stop my heart.
I will leave my uneasiness
To the waters
And the stars!

NIGHT WATCH

What is left of that night watch
Since I lost everything!

The full moon remains
With the shudders of solitude
And the plains
That long for the dawn.

Sadness remains in the heart
And an inclement fate.

I have lost you,
I will lament till dawn to the full moon:
What a night,
What a pitiable night!

REED GRASS

The fogs of fall
Will cover the stars,
Impenetrable quagmires
Will cover the clearest lakes.
And no one will see
How the reeling reed grass
Was dumbfounded in the dark.

Space is blind,
Depths are blind —
Complete darkness
Has covered my earth and sky —
How sad you are,
Oh, reed grass, seeing clearly
With the eyes of lakes and stars!

28

THE ASTRONAUT

I don't think I'll live to see
The first astronaut
Who will see the stars
In the timeless cosmos.
When he comes back
I will have made my own journey
Into space
From which no one
Returns.

When he talks
About Alpha Centauri,
About light years
In constellation nebulas —
I will have long since
Stopped speaking
And will have turned
Into a wandering piece of dust
In the cosmic night.

The crowds in joy will carry
The astronaut in their arms,
They'll keep his spacesuit
In a museum.
But the wind also
Joyfully carries the leaves —
Carries the holy remains
Of summer . . .

I can be a piece of dust
In the expanse of the sky,
I can be a leaf
In the captivity of fall.
I know who owns this
Great universe —
The leaf,
Dust, autumn,
Constellations, wind.

DUSK

Only three small stars
Hang low in the sky.
Fog rises from the fearful waters,
My home drifts into darkness.

How can I live, how can I love and die
With those three stars —
How can I offer my heart to the sunrise?

The path is black and the trees are black —
I cannot see a thing;
But I know who prays that I rest easy
On the other side of night.

THE OBSERVATION

Let's wait until
The joker poet Li Po
Comes down the path of the sharp hills
To joke with the moon.

The gates in the yard creak open —
The forests do not feel his steps.
Li Po walks softly
Carrying a cup brimming with wine.

Let's wait — soon his shadow
Will nod in the loft
Like a lotus blossom
Bobbing on the lake waves.

Let's listen — soon the poet
Will ask the moon to drink
His joy or sadness
From the brimming cup.

LIGHTS

Again the night
Opened my eyes —
I watch the evening lights,
And they seem clearer
In the water
Than in a window.

They are real ropes of gold —
But who will tie me with them
To the lights
That never dim in windows
And never die
In the ocean depths?

This harbor
Is a black window
Swollen with crystalline lights.
I search for one small gleam
In the water
But do not find it.

IN THE COFFIN

There are no cracks in the coffin
For light to enter —
Whoever made my coffin
Loved night more
Than the dawn.

Light breaks up
The thickest clouds —
From these coffin boards reflect
The smiles of the stars and sun.

When the
Sunset-blinded ponds
Regain their sight at dawn —
Will I see you
In the water lily?

34

BETRAYAL

The stars tonight are so cold —
They do not revive the heart
With their light
Or heat
As if they had been hammered
From those silver coins
That once lured Judas
For your betrayal.

You are again betrayed somewhere,
Again kissed by Judas
For the tempting false glitter
Of silver.
Otherwise the heavens would not be black
And the full moon so saddened —
Otherwise the stars would not shake
All night with cold
In the skies above the poplar.

OPEN YOUR EYES

You don't see the brightness of the sun
Or feel the glow of love,
And you wonder why the full moon
Looks so angrily at you.

And why shouldn't it stare,
How could it not condemn such blindness?
You — splinter of the morning star —
Open your eyes, open your eyes!

36

LET'S LOOK

Let's look straight
At the greatness of the stars,
Raising our eyes from the dewed fields.
It's said that they glow for you,
Insect of the earth.

But is it for us to know
What art that is,
What learning lies beyond the night sky,
And in which galaxy live
God's nations.

37

Shores of oblivion

MONUMENT VALLEY

Numberless monuments
Without inscriptions . . .
I carry your name, eternal love,
In my heart.

There are so many lives here,
Scratched into stone —
You sing in pain,
Engraved within me.

If you know who made those letters,
Do not reveal it.
My heart's blood
Drips from the chiseled lines.

41

THE TOMB

A hill of white ice rose
In the north sea
Like a marble tomb.
And I wondered what thing fierce fate
Had closed up so tightly
In that tomb.

No name is carved there,
No merits listed.
How can I guess
Whose cold body rests there —
Whose remains travel
To the shores of oblivion.

There is no cross on the tomb.
No initials of eternal rest
Carved on the ice slab.
I pray that I'll be able
To sing a lament
For the dead with the ocean waves.

EXISTENCE

You don't care that the wind will scatter
The blood foam in the seas without a trace —
You've locked yourself into your tranquil life
Like the insect in yellow amber.

Don't believe that rocks by the sea
No longer will sweat blood —
The nine-headed dragon looks down to earth
And awaits his hour.

It may be possible to guard ourselves,
To kill that dragon with a lance.
Thoughts and fancies have not yet jelled,
The stones still pray for us.

43

PELICANS

Pelicans, deliberations finished,
Glide on my wings.
It's time to say: Until we meet again
To the palmtree shore.

What we saw — we saw,
What we heard — we heard — enough!
Twilight glides on pelican wings,
The sun sinks into the sea.

44

THE WINDOW

Your hands covered my window
With bricks of cloud.
I will not see how waves bluster
With storms in the ocean.

I will hear only the drone
That makes the stones weep.
All the ruined waves
Will break against my heart.

45

LIFE

Do not look at my life —
The tomb of Tutankhamun —
God's secret shrouds and protects it
Like the pyramid a body
From your stares.

Do not enter the dark
To plunder my treasure.
May the blackened mummy —
Man's youth —
Decay in the smelted gold
Of the summer sunset.

There on the wall are
The unreadable signs —
Man, beast and bird.
They glorify
The black mummy's
Golden shell.

46

Along the border walls are things
Untouched by death
That we will never use.
They will present you
With protected life's
Nameless riddle.

Oh, the same life,
The same death
In the atomic age
And the 18th dynasty!
Do not look at your brother
Tutankhamun's face
In scorn.

47

LEGENDARY BELLS

On the shore dry grasses
And in the lake, bells!
Wind, you became my brother
Long ago.

When they began to ring
We both awakened
And in the autumn rage
Torment ourselves with leaves.

Should we chase them
Through the empty fields?
O Lord, my wits —
We left the bells!

The bells that woke us,
The bells that will
Put us, the stones
And the waves in the lake to sleep.

48

THE BLACK BIRD

It's already a good half hour after six,
Day has dived into evening,
And our heartaches will not echo
In the stunned forest trees.

The black bird fluttered by —
We saw the wings of the demon.
The black terror twisted
The chestnut trees on the hill.

Open up, gates of triumph,
When you hear the bells of victory.
Slaves, cry out in joy
On the awakening graves!

MY MOTHER

I.

I watched you
As you threaded the amber
And decorated your hair with flowers.
In the beauty of your adornment
I still see summers playing
With the rainbows of dawn,
Plenitudes of blossoms.

You explained that
Witches weave rainbows,
The earth gives birth to flowers without pain —
I saw happiness in your smile:
The colors of the rainbow,
The joy of the flower.

But when the wind
Howled in from the seas
I saw fear again in your eyes.
You hurried to thread the amber,
Finish your stories
And plait your braids —
Faster, faster . . .

II.

As the sun returns
To rest in the sea,
So you returned.
Each day, thinking of the shores of your birth,
Your face gleamed
With the colors of sunset.

You didn't seem to be yourself,
Singing of the waves —
The setting sun warmed your songs,
The storm shook loose the waves,
And I remained
A martyr of the memories of childhood

And I too
Was uneasy
When the sea-winds howled.
I watched you
Near the shattered amber home —
You stood in my eyes
Like a goddess of the seas . . .

51

III.

I am indeed
A martyr of the memories of childhood,
Though my face hides my secret well —
Perhaps only that Baltic wave
Knows my heartache,
Perhaps only that ocean wind . . .

I believe with my whole heart
That rivers are the daughters of the sea
And lakes, the sons.
Nothing clouded my young convictions,
Not the restless sea,
Not the terrible ocean whirlwind.

And I would not trade
My mother's belief:
The power of song, the truth of stories
In the amber castle of the sea goddess,
In the majesty of stormy seas.

THE STONE

If the bird
Doesn't recognize his last year's nest
Despite the plenitude of dry stalks —
How will you, man, after this storm
Recognize your home
From one remaining stone?

Stone does not differ from stone —
They are all alike: all cold.
And our hearthstone will be as cold
As a heart torn long ago
From a flaming breast.

53

SNOWFLAKE

I don't separate the blossoms from the snowflakes —
They are both white.
Spring ended long ago,
Summer flourished.
Then autumn took away
The blossoms and the leaves.
Now it's winter —
Again I rock you, little snowflake,
In my hand.

Again I sing the Lullaby —
Do you hear it?
Today the pinewoods will sing only
Christ's heartache
And the cedar branches will not rock you.
My palm will be
Your only cradle —
Rest there
Until we melt together
In the smile of the sun.

BLOSSOMS

I am only a visitor;
My brothers, blossoms.
Chills shake my bones
Beneath these black robes.

The frosts fell too early
On the sunfilled lawns
And on songs written down
With the blood of my earth.

The frozen ground will lock up our hearts —
We will die, brothers blossoms.
I beneath the black cassock,
You beneath the northern ice.

THE SEAGULL

Stop, stop as you fly by —
We will sit together on this rock.
The Almighty made this endless sea
And those far shores for both of us.

There is enough room on this rock;
It will suffice for both to rest.
We can take pleasure in the full horizon
And the hills of water that glow in the sunset.

IF YOU CAME BACK

How lucky I would be
If you came back to me —
The yard, the house, the old books
Would smell of chamomile.

The lindens in the middle
Of the yard would rustle happily
If they knew it was you
Who hid my stories.

Oh, I know that they were left behind
Where the frosts never end,
Where among the wreaths of mourning
Are born the song and pain.

AUTUMN

I remember that autumn
When the fallen epileptic maple
Shuddered in pain
By the road.
My world died then
With the maple's first convulsion.
And your last
Grassland butterflies, Lord,
Died too.

I scorned that autumn,
Ignored its power,
And in vengeance
It mercilessly raged.
Now each year bird swarms
Hurry to funerals
Though I am already buried —
The butterflies in the grasslands,
The maples by the road
Are rigid.
Now each year bird swarms
Bind up the heavens
With black wreaths.

VIOLIN

The grasshoppers will lose their heads —
It will be hard for men to keep still . . .
And I will play your violin,
Francis of Assisi.

And I will try to be a grasshopper,
Mad with the joys of summer.
Beneath the Lord's blue canopy
Soul abounds with grace and love.

But can we wait for miracles
When the violin is but frail wood
And the songs in the gardens end
As birds wing to the skies?

If sometimes I play out of tune
And the violin strings cry out in pain —
Remember that I am just a grasshopper,
A summer player, before my death.

WILL HE KNOW

When the bird, sated with seeds,
Does not find water in the stone crack —
Will he know
Where my rivers flow,
Lakes lie?

Will he know what it means in a drought
To be without one's rivers and lakes?
Will he know,
Will he feel
That my heartache
Can eat away the stones?

60

FRIEND

I have not found a better friend
Than the saguaro in the sun's valley.
Saguaro, I think of you
Here in the sunset near the sea.

As if you had become a part of me,
I feel the same uneasiness
When the blood-colored horizon
Presses down against the cactus.

You remained alone in the distance,
Your arms raised high,
Where my footprints were covered
By the wild desert sands.

You remained beyond the sun's altar,
Among the endless windstorms,
On the other side of night and dawn —
In the memories of a wanderer . . .

O, how can I call out for you
When my longing tosses across the waves
And seagulls prophesy the end
Of our eternal friendship?

THE VOICE OF VYTAUTAS
THE GREAT (XV CENTURY)

I

My treasure —
Two seas,
The fertile plains,
The bright clear sky,
A million melodic skylarks,
Trees, rivers, waves.

In my solitude I cry out:
To whom will I leave my treasure,
I have not sired a son —
For whom will my beloved seas moan,
For whom will the skylarks sing,
Rivers flood,
Oceans drone?

All crossroads
Once led to glory
But the future now inspires only pain —
I haven't see my face in my son's,
I haven't heard my voice in his —
And I sit and curse all treasures.

63

II

I will sleep with the hope of triumph
Like the hearth —
With one glowing ember,
And will dream through the severe night
That I flame
With fire for Lithuania.

I wore no wreath on my head,
I did not hold a king's scepter in my hand —
The barren nights did not give birth to morning,
Did not stir the embers
In the ashes into flame . . .

Biting winds will tear my dreams
Like a flag raised high on the battlefield;
The embers of my fire
Will wander through cold eternity
Until they regain their heat
In your hearts.

FAREWELL

In an hour
Our visit will be over.
Let's press our hands together,
Bid each other farewell
While the candle still flickers.

We cannot wait
Another minute —
The raised sails whisper to the clouds,
The winds have revived after three days —
We have to be on time!

This is no place for tears,
Fainting spells, or panic —
We have an hour to bid farewell!
A minute longer would sink us
Like icebergs the Titanic.

Children, do not caress
Your mothers long,
Friends and lovers, laugh,
And remember
Your love is just beginning.

The swelling sails,
The awakening winds
Call us out to sail the peaceful seas
Unexplored by Vikings, Argonauts,
Or Odysseyans . . .

ACKNOWLEDGMENTS

Rivers, Night Watch, and *Reed Grass* first appeared in *Rapport* 10, published in Pittsburgh by The Slow Loris Press. I thank the editors for their permission to republish the poems in this collection. I also wish to thank the Connecticut Commission on the Arts for a grant which enabled me to prepare this manuscript for publication.

J. Z.